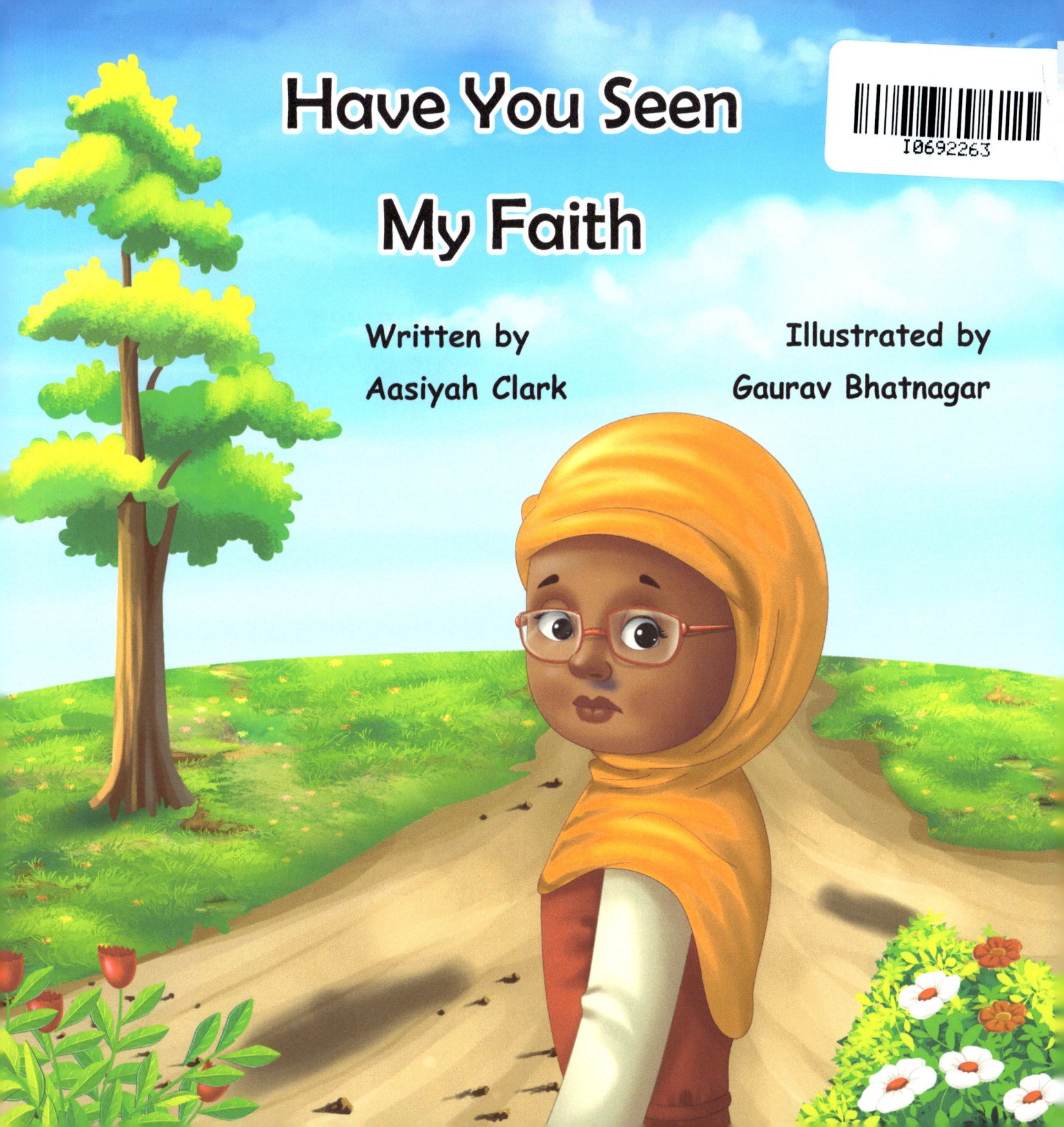

Have You Seen My Faith

Written by
Aasiyah Clark

Illustrated by
Gaurav Bhatnagar

ISBN:978-1-7366736-0-7 (Paperback)
978-1-7366736-1-4 (eBook)

Illustrated and designed by Gaurav Bhatnagar
www.ePublishingexperts.com

Dedicated to My Sweetness, Dr. Abdul-Ghaffaar and to My Little loves, Ihsan & Ibrahim

Mama, have you seen my faith?

They told me that I lost it.

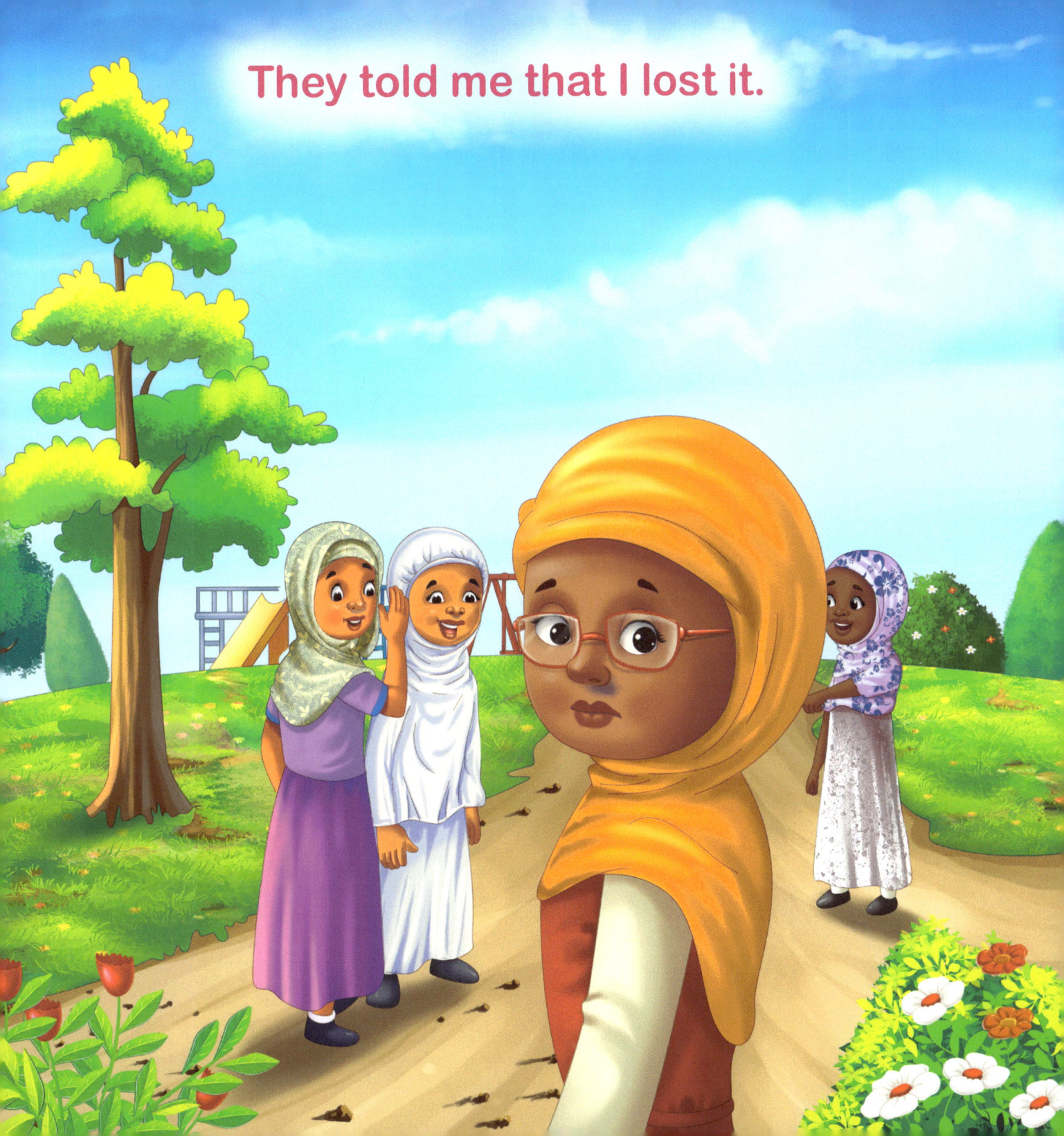

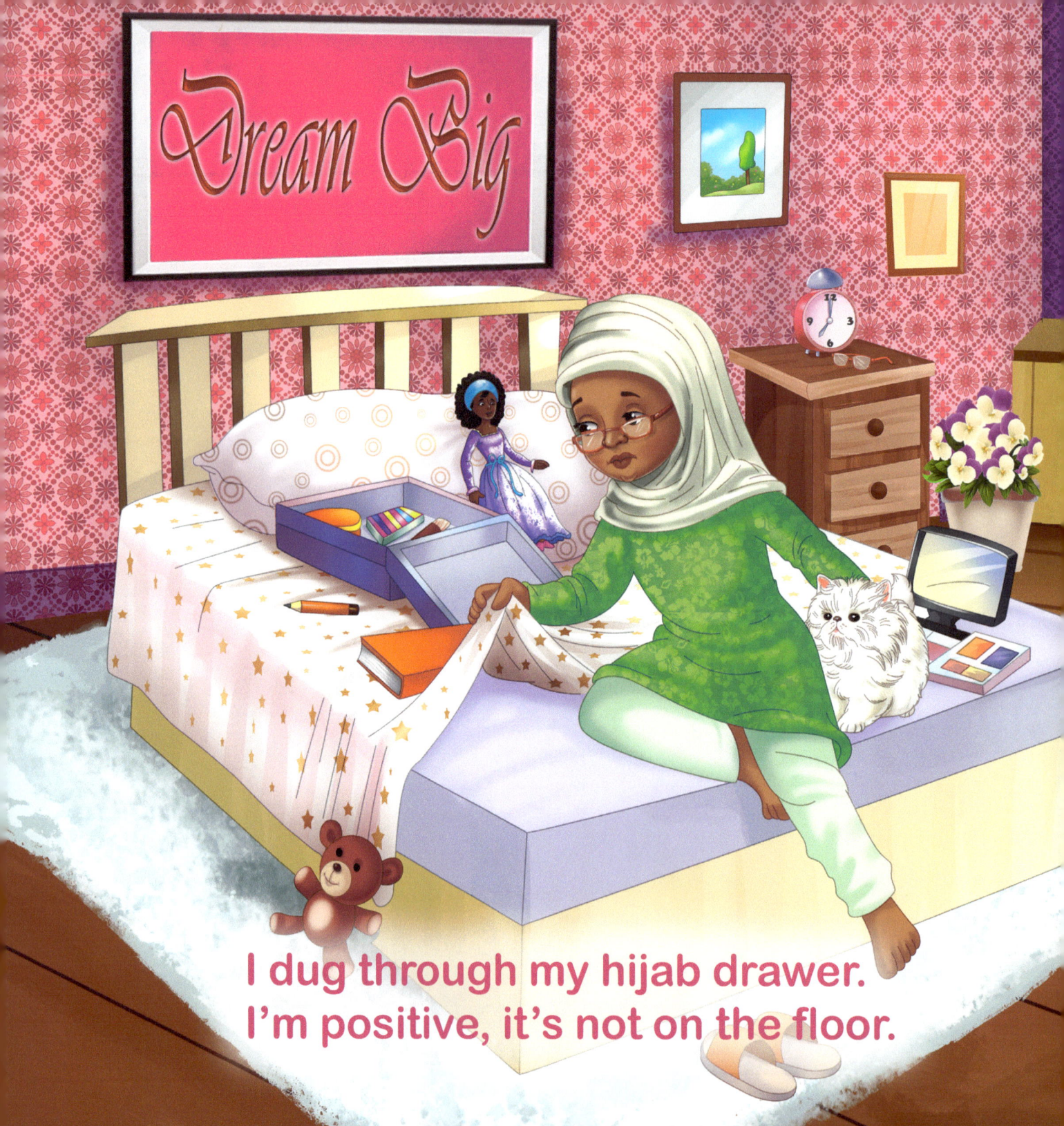

I dug through my hijab drawer.
I'm positive, it's not on the floor.

I searched the couch cushions,
looked under my bed.
Somehow, I misplaced it… at least that's
what they said.

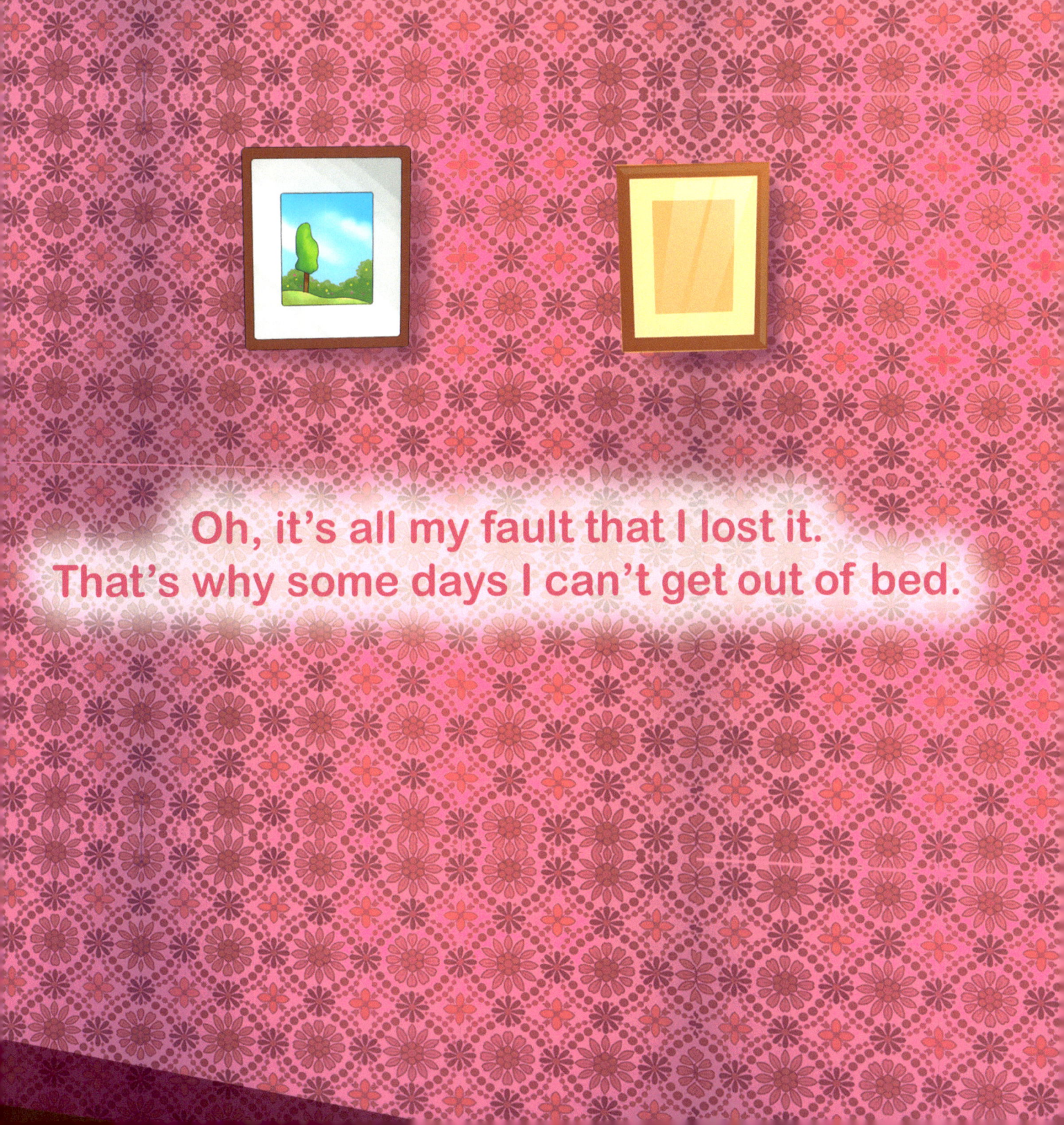

Oh, it's all my fault that I lost it.
That's why some days I can't get out of bed.

If only I could remember where I left it,
I could get this sadness out my head.

Will you help me find my faith?

So I can show it off.

I'm told that once I find my faith,
all my problems will be solved.

I'll finally have some friends,
and won't worry hardly at all.

Oh, Aisha, your faith isn't lost.
It's not something to be found.
At least not under the sofa, it's
not just laying around.

We can pray and practice the Sunnah.

There are specific duaa we can say.
But my love, depression is real,
and seeking counsel is
the Islamic way.

I'll tell you what we'll do, we'll find a therapist...

who will teach us new skills that will work for you.

We can have faith,
and a therapist too.

Strong faith isn't a choice to be made between the two.